Dear Parents and Teachers,

In an easy-reader format, **My Readers** introduce classic stories to children who are learning to read. Favorite characters and time-tested tales are the basis for **My Readers**, which are available in three levels:

1   **Level One** is for the emergent reader and features repetitive language and word clues in the illustrations.

2   **Level Two** is for more advanced readers who still need support saying and understanding some words. Stories are longer with word clues in the illustrations.

3   **Level Three** is for independent, fluent readers who enjoy working out occasional unfamiliar words. The stories are longer and divided into chapters.

Encourage children to select books based on interests, not reading levels. Read aloud with children, showing them how to use the illustrations for clues. With adult guidance and rereading, children will eventually read the desired book on their own.

Here are some ways you might want to use this book with children:

- Talk about the title and the cover illustrations. Encourage the child to use these to predict what the story is about.
- Discuss the interior illustrations and try to piece together a story based on the pictures. Does the child want to change or adjust his first prediction?
- After children reread a story, suggest they retell or act out a favorite part.

My Readers will not only help children become readers, they will serve as an introduction to some of the finest classic children's books available today.

—LAURA ROBB
Educator and Reading Consultant

For activities and reading tips, visit myreadersonline.com.

To my mother, Vera,
and
my mother-in-law, Marge,
with love and admiration

SQUARE
FISH
An Imprint of Macmillan Children's Publishing Group

Library of Congress Cataloging-in-Publication Data
Seeger, Laura Vaccaro.
Dog and Bear / by Laura Vaccaro Seeger.
p.   cm.
"A Neal Porter Book"
Summary: Three easy-to-read stories reveal the close friendship between Dog and Bear.
contents: Bear in the chair—Play with me! Play with me!—Dog changes his name.
[Best friends—Fiction. 2. Friendship—Fiction. 3. Dogs—Fiction. 4. Bears—Fiction.] I. Title.
PZ7.S4514Dog 2007   [E]—dc22   t 2006011687

ISBN 978-0-312-64171-9 (hardcover)
1 3 5 7 9 10 8 6 4 2

ISBN 978-0-312-54799-8 (paperback)
1 3 5 7 9 10 8 6 4 2

Book design by Patrick Collins/Véronique Lefèvre Sweet

Square Fish logo designed by Filomena Tuosto

Originally published: Roaring Brook Press, 2007
First My Readers Edition: 2012

myreadersonline.com
mackids.com

This is a Level 2 book

AR: 1.3 / LEXILE: AD320L

Dog and Bear

TWO FRIENDS, THREE STORIES

Laura Vaccaro Seeger

SQUARE
FISH

Macmillan Children's Publishing Group

New York

Bear in the Chair

"Is that you, Bear?"

"Yes, Dog."

"It is a beautiful day," said Dog.

"Come outside with me."

"I can't get down," said Bear.

"Just jump."

"But I am scared!"

"Not to worry, Bear. I will help you."

"Come closer.

You can slide down my back."

"You can do it," said Dog.

Bear was more frightened than ever.

Dog said, "Take one step.

One little, tiny step."

"Now, take one more."

With each step, Bear became braver.

Finally, Bear reached Dog.

"Whee! That was fun!"

"Good. Now we can go out," said Dog.

"Where is your scarf?"

"Uh-oh," said Bear.

"Maybe we should just

stay inside," said Dog.

"Bear, will you play
with me?"
"Not right now, Dog.
I am reading my book."

"Please, Bear. Play with me."

"I am reading a story

about a dog and a stuffed bear."

"Oh, Bear. Play with me!"

"In this book,
the dog and the bear
are best friends."

"Come on, Bear.

Play with me!"

"Although they love to be together,
sometimes the bear just needs time
to himself," said Bear.

"Play with me! Play with me!"

"Play with me! Play with me!"

"The bear tried

to explain this to the dog,

but the dog did not understand,"

Bear continued.

"Play with me! Play with me!"

"After a while, the bear realized
that the dog just wanted
to be with his friend," said Bear.

"All right, Dog.

I will play with you now.

What shall we do?"

"Read to me! Read to me!"

Fido

Dog Changes

His Name

Duke

Rover

"I am changing my name," said Dog.

"But why, Dog?"

"Because DOG is b-o-r-i-n-g!

From now on, call me SPOT."

"But you don't have any spots."

"What about FLUFFY?" said Dog.

"You are not fluffy."

"Well, how about PRINCE?"

"Oh, no," said Bear.

"SKIPPY?"

Bear smiled.

"ZIPPY?"

Bear thought for a moment.

"How about MY BEST FRIEND DOG?"
said Bear.

"I like that!" said Dog.

"Or just DOG for short!"

"Perfect," said Bear.